Mookie Goes Down the Shore

Written by Mookie San West
Typed by Judith Kristen
Illustrated by Sue V. Daly

Judith Kristen & S. Daly

Copyright 2009, Aquinas & Krone Publishing, LLC. All rights reserved.

No part of this book may be reproduced, stored in a retrieval system, or transmitted by any means without written permission from the publisher.

First published by Aquinas & Krone Publishing, LLC 5/24/2009.

ISBN # 978-0-9800448-6-7

Printed in the United States of America.

This book is printed on acid-free paper.

Cover illustration by Sue V. Daly.
Please feel welcome to visit www.illustrationsbySueDaly.com & JudithKristen.com

Sue V. Daly's photo taken by Shauna L. Daly.
Mookie's photo by Jonathan Reed West.
Cover design by Tim Litostansky.
Mookie's hat courtesy of Fran Fredman.

This book is dedicated to
Anna and John Turner.

Hi…it's me, Mookie! Let's go down the shore! Yup, that's what I said… "down the shore." That's what *everyone* who lives in New Jersey says. They never say, "Let's go to the beach."

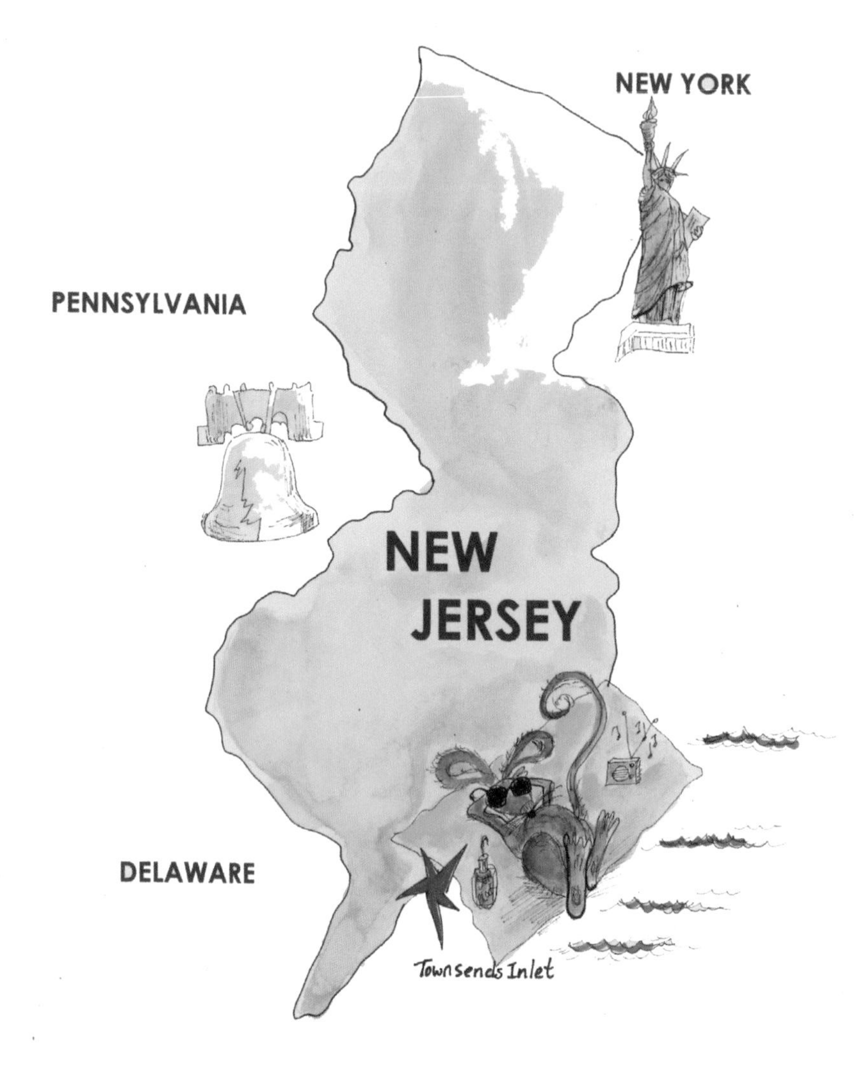

The place we live 'down the shore' for a part of every summer is in a lovely little town connected to Sea Isle City.

It's called Townsends Inlet.

Last year we lived in a big house right near the old drawbridge that connects Townsends Inlet to another lovely little town called Avalon.

When we arrived, all eight of us: Mom, Dad, me, Holly, Ned, Cynthia, Miss Rose, and of course, our Sheepdog Henley, well, we just fell in love with the place!

The minute we entered the house, all of my cat friends left their cages and jumped up onto the front windowsill to see the view from our beautiful vacation home.

The first thing Mom and Dad did was put the groceries away.

In the meantime, Henley and I found a dog door in the kitchen. It was too small for a dog as big as our Henley. But it wasn't too small for a cat like me!

I quickly ran into the living room and hopped up onto the windowsill to spread the good news.

"A door?! Are you kidding me?!" Rose shook her head. "Have you looked outside this window yet?"

"Well, no, but…"

"*Well*," Holly interrupted, "there's not much out there to entertain a cat, Mookie."

Ned agreed. "She's right ya know, just sand and some water. That's about it."

“And anyway,” Cynthia spoke up, “we’re housecats…or did you forget that?!”

I sighed and left the window without saying another word.

Henley passed by me on his way upstairs and gave me a loving nudge. "About that dog door out in the kitchen," he said to me.

I looked at him ever so innocently. "Oh, is that what it was?"

"Listen, I'm not worried about the other cats, but *you*, Adventure Boy…stay away from it."

"Why?" (again with my innocent face)

"Because it leads outside and you don't know anything about seashore life or what goes on out there."

“Ah, don’t worry about me,” I said as we walked into the dining room together. “The five of us already had our ‘cat talk.’ There’s nothin’ out there but sand and some water. Come here! Have a look for yourself.”

Henley never said anything after I showed him that. I guess he believed me.

…Silly dog.

The kitchen was just about ten feet away from where I stood in the dining room and so I trekked in there to investigate the dog door.

I sniffed at it and then pushed my paw against some sort of rubbery flap.

"WOO-HOO!!! This leads right outside! No screen…no other doors…just a small rubber flap between me and Mother Nature!"

My curiosity got the best of me. I pushed the flap open once again and stepped outside onto the big back deck! I immediately smelled the fresh ocean air and felt a nice cool breeze wrap itself around me.

I ran down the steps, scampered out toward the front of the house, and then climbed on top of a HUGE sand dune - surveying my new domain. I felt like King of the Hill!

I soon decided that it was time for the "King" to move on and before I knew it I found myself right under our front steps. I sniffed around a bit and felt pretty sure it was safe to move on.

I ran out about ten or fifteen feet and then turned around to see Ned, Cynthia, Holly, and Rose all staring at me from the front window. I heard Miss Rose holler, "YOU CRAZY CAT! GET BACK IN HERE!"

I smiled and waved my paw, but I had *no* plans to go back in the house – not just yet. I wanted to take a little stroll to see what was *really* going on at the shore besides just "sand and some water."

As I walked over another sand dune or two I spotted something very strange on the beach. It was a Horseshoe Crab! It looked like a cross between an old tin can, a hubcap, and a small dinosaur. It kinda scared me…but not really.

Then I decided to walk down toward the water. Now that was interesting!

I saw all kinds of pretty shells, dark green seaweed, and some really cute little creatures living inside their very own shell houses. They were Hermit Crabs!

When I moved in for a closer look they all hid inside their homes. I sniffed one of the larger shells and a tiny voice squeaked at me. "Go away, cat…or you'll be sorry!"

I figured I'd better take the hint.

No sooner had I walked over a very large sand dune when I spied *another crab* - a blue crab. And he didn't like me one bit!

"WHAT ARE YOU DOING HERE?!" he yelled as he clicked his pincers together. "Where are your manners?! This is no place for a cat…now shoo…SCAT…**SCRAM**!!"

"You know…you've got a *real* crabby disposition," I smiled.

"Crabby, huh? I suppose you think that's funny? Well, it's not! It's not one *bit* funny, Mr. Smarty Pants!"

I laughed to myself and ran as fast as I could to the other side of a nearby sand dune.

I quickly caught my breath and then continued my walk down the beach. Suddenly, a bird called a seagull landed right in front of me.

Now in the world I come from, birds are afraid of cats. But NOT down the shore...and definitely not *this* bird!

"What are *you* doing here?!" his big voice squawked at me.

"Me? I'm on an adventure trip!"

"I see," he said giving me the once over. "So apparently you're not your typical house-cat from the big city."

I puffed my chest out proudly. "Nope. I'm sure not typical. And you're not the kind of bird I'm used to seeing in the city either. You're cool with me." I smiled. "I like that!"

"Well," he said strutting around me, "that's 'cause I'm a big, strong shore bird *and*…I can always fly away if I have to."

I looked at my new friend and smiled once again.

He started to flap his long, feathery wings. “I gotta go, young fella. Time for breakfast on the bay! See ya later, kid!”

Just as he was taking flight I said, “Hey! Mr. Seagull! What’s your name? Mine’s Mookie!”

“Bernie,” he said. His voice was fading as he flew higher into the clear blue sky. “Just call me Bernie.”

"Bernie Seagull," I smiled. "Nice name."

I looked up again to see that Bernie had joined some of his other seagull friends. They were all flying toward the bay. I decided to run down the beach and watch them fly. I think flying is so cool. Don't you?

Soon Bernie and his friends were almost out of sight and I sat there right at the edge of the water looking out upon the Townsends Inlet/Avalon Bridge.

The water was a deep greenish-blue color and the light from the early afternoon sun sparkled on it like diamonds. It was very pretty.

Just then I saw some GIANT fish almost fly out of the water. I sat there and counted them: 1,2,3,4,5,6,7,8! One of them swam about ten feet away from me…and she had a big smile on her face.

"You know, I *never* saw a fish who was happy to see a cat!" I smiled back.

"That's because I'm a dolphin! My name is Marina. Actually, I'm a mammal, not a fish."

"Oh," I said softly.

"Dolphins always smile!" she said splashing her fins in the water.

Then Marina turned and rejoined her Dolphin family. All of them looked back at me…smiling. How sweet is that?!

Soon after Marina and her family swam away I heard a very loud horn. I immediately turned toward the sound. It was a fishing boat!

It was filled with nets, rods, reels, life preservers, and of course, fishermen.

One of them called out, "Hey there, little fella! We'll be back around 4:30! I'll save you a nice, big fish!" He laughed and then waved at me.

I watched as the boat powered its way out of my sight and then I heard *another* voice. It was a little girl with her Mom and Dad, carrying a big umbrella, a blanket, and some beach toys.

"Mommy! Daddy! Look! A kittie! I think he's lost! Can we take him home with us? Can we? Can we, please?! Pretty, pretty please!!!"

Just as the little girl was about to pick me up, I side-stepped and then scampered away as fast as I could right back toward our beach house. I'm sure that she and her parents would have given me a really nice home, but I was more than happy with the family I already had.

I knew my way back to the beach house - thanks to my outstanding feline instincts. I ran over my "King of the Hill" sand dune, up the back steps, and then straight through my little "Mookie Door." As far as I was concerned it was no longer a dog door.

Miss Rose, Holly, Ned, and Cynthia had obviously seen me run toward the house and they greeted me the minute I flew in through the little rubber entryway.

"Well, Adventure Cat," Rose sniffed at me, "how was it out there?"

Holly looked at my sandy, wet paws. “Looks to me like *exactly* what we said it would be - just sand and some water.”

I turned and walked away from all four of them.

"Yup," I smiled. "You were right. Nothin' at all out there but sand and some water. …Nothin' at all."

Have a Happy Summer!!!

The End

. . . for now

Legend has it that a small orange tabby cat was seen strolling the boardwalk in Sea Isle City. It has been said that he was also: chasing a few seagulls, napping on top of the lifeguard stand, and attempting to steal a chicken and tomato sandwich out of a well-stocked picnic basket on the 85th Street beach.

(Now just who do you think that could have been?!)

Sue V. Daly is an award-winning illustrator specializing in pen and ink drawings. She graduated from the University of Pennsylvania, Kutztown, with a degree in Advertising Art. Sue has two daughters, Lauren and Shauna. She now lives outside Chicago with her husband Bill and her two adorable beagles, Corky and Dude. Sue is also the proud grand mom of darling twins, Emma and Andrew.